MERIDIAN™

Flying Solo

Chapter 1

CREATORS

Barbara Kesel
Writer

Joshua Middleton
Penciler

Dexter Vines
Inker

Michael Atiyeh
Colorist

Dave Lanphear
Letterer

MERIDIAN #5
Paul Mounts
Colorist

MERIDIAN #5 cover:
Joshua Middleton
Penciler
Dexter Vines
Inker
Michael Atiyeh
Colorist

MERIDIAN #6
Joshua Middleton
with Steve McNiven
Pencilers
Dexter Vines
with John Dell
Inkers
Morry Hollowell
Colorist

MERIDIAN #6 cover:
Joshua Middleton
Penciler
Dexter Vines
Inker
Michael Atiyeh
Colorist

MERIDIAN #7
Steve McNiven
Penciler
Jordi Ensign
Inker
Morry Hollowell
Colorist

CROSSGEN CHRONICLES #1
Ron Marz
with Barbara Kesel
Writers
Claudio Castellini
Penciler
Caesar Rodriguez
with Andrew Crossley
CG Inkers
Michael Atiyeh
Colorist

The CrossGen Universe created by Mark Alessi & Gina M. Villa

TRADE PAPERBACK

Cover Painted by Steve Rude

DESIGN
Pam Davies
Dave Lanphear
Brandon Peterson
Sylvia Bretz
Troy Peteri

EDITORIAL
Tony Panaccio
Ian M. Feller
Michael A. Beattie
Barbara Kesel
Mark Waid
Bart Sears
Gina M. Villa

Meridian™: Flying Solo Vol. 1, MAY 2001. FIRST PRINTING. Originally published in single magazine form as Meridian™ Vol. 1, Issues #1-7. Copyright © 2000, 2001. All rights reserved. Published by CrossGeneration Comics, Inc. Office of publication: 4023 Tampa Road, Suite 2400, Oldsmar, Florida 34677. CrossGen®, CrossGen Comics® and CrossGeneration Comics® are registered trademarks of CrossGeneration Comics, Inc. Meridian™, the CrossGen sigil™, and all prominent characters are ™ and © 2001 CrossGeneration Comics, Inc. All rights reserved. The entire contents of this book are ™ and © 2001 CrossGeneration Comics, Inc. The stories, incidents, and characters in this publication are fictional. Any similarities to persons living or dead are purely coincidental. With the exception of artwork used for review purposes, none of the contents of this book may be reproduced in any form without the express written consent of CrossGeneration Comics, Inc. PRINTED IN CANADA.

FOREWORD

> *"The female of the species*
> *is more deadly than the male."*
> **Rudyard Kipling**

This one would be the showstopper. You see, we knew that creating CrossGeneration Comics from scratch would be one heck of a trick. On the surface, it seemed positively absurd.

We were setting out to start a brand new comic book publishing company in a sliding marketplace. We wouldn't do superheroes, the best-selling genre in the history of the medium. We wouldn't employ variant covers, crossovers and other marketing gimmicks, as these devices were in direct conflict with our principles and our long-term plan for rebuilding the audience for comic books. We would even offer a money-back guarantee for the first few issues of the monthly comic books just to make absolutely certain that everyone in this industry would have every possible reason to question our mental health.

But *Meridian* would be the exclamation point at the end of that declaration. It would be a comic book about a girl.

And it wouldn't be about boyfriends and make-up and the prom. It would be an adventure story set against the backdrop of political intrigue and financial maneuvering, where the real power is actually manifested i the real world. Our hero wouldn't have the body proportions of a professional wrestler or wear a Spandex outfit or even know martial arts. She would be a normal, awkwar tomboyish, spunky teen-age girl named Seph

When you think about it, we had to do a book like *Meridian*. CrossGen's primary mission, above all else, was to inject some new life into this incredible, time-honored y recently-maligned artform known as comic books. How else could we do this unless we re-enfranchised a sector of the population that once was a pillar of support in the com book business: girls!

Back in the 50s, 60s and 70s, Archie Comics, marketed largely toward young girls were incredibly popular, selling competitivel with mainstream superhero comics such as *Superman*, *Batman* and *Spider-Man*. Howeve in recent years those demographics had changed; young girls had become a small fraction of the comics audience, in large par because most publishers geared their efforts towards an audience made up primarily of 10- to 24-year-old males. Worse, the industry wasn't bringing in many new young readers, male or female.

We were determined to come up with a

concept interesting enough to draw girls back into buying comics again, so we came up with a few rules:

• **It had to be smart.** One of the reasons girls weren't reading comics anymore was because the few comics that had been marketed to them were old-fashioned in their simplicity. We couldn't run the risk of "dumbing things down" for a new, more sophisticated generation. If anything, we had to write a story that would challenge today's readers.

• **The art had to be different.** We couldn't publish a book for a different audience with a different story with a different lead character and expect it to look like every other comic book on the stand. The art had to reflect the sensibilities and the emotions of the characters. Since we weren't going to have super-powered, muscular Spandex jockeys duking it out with super-villains, then we needed to be able to portray the reduction of physical action in an engaging and exciting manner. Since much of the story initially would involve political intrigue, we needed to make sure that it could be presented dynamically and stylishly.

• **We couldn't make it look _too_ different.** In order for *Meridian* to succeed, we had to entice girl readers without driving male

readers away, so the book had to move and flow well. There needed to be some action, some danger, and some adventure to be certain that we wouldn't lose the attention of the traditional comic book audience.

• **We couldn't make Sephie too powerful.** Of course, as with all of CrossGen's initial four titles — *Mystic, Sigil, Scion* and *Meridian* — the Sigil would be a factor. For the uninitiated, the Sigil is an imprint of power randomly bestowed upon certain characters in our universe. Our stories of heroes who are coming of age or coming to responsibility center around how they use that power, how it is manifested, and how it affects their lives and their worlds. In *Meridian*, we have two Sigil-Bearers: Sephie and Ilahn, Sephie's uncle and Minister of the neighboring city of Cadador. Ilahn balances Sephie's influence over her world, forcing Sephie to take up the mantle of reluctant hero. How those two conflict and the consequences brought by their battle is the center of *Meridian*'s story.

But I don't want to give the punchline away. This is Sephie's tale. Best to let her tell it. ☯

MARK

Mark Alessi

THIS PLACE GROWS COLDER, MY FRIEND. ITS ENERGY WANES. I AM SEEKING A SOLUTION, AND EAGERLY WELCOME YOUR THOUGHTS.

IT IS NOT LIKE YOU TO BE SO TROUBLED.

SO LONG AGO, WHEN IT WAS ALL SET IN MOTION, IT WAS SO... FASCINATING IN ITS COMPLEXITY. IT SURPRISED EVEN ME. NOW THINGS ARE STATIC, WORLDS GROW COLD, AND WHAT WERE ONCE GLORIOUS FIELDS OF BATTLE LAY STILL AND BARREN.

THE PROBLEM IS NOT SIMPLY LAZY WARRIORS. THE VITAL ENERGIES ON WHICH WE ALL DEPEND ARE FADING AWAY... IT SHOULDN'T HAPPEN LIKE THIS... YET IT IS! IT IS DYING, AND THE FIRST DO NOTHING TO PREVENT IT!

BECAUSE THE FIRST DON'T UNDERSTAND. THEY HAVE NO IDEA OF THE CONNECTION BETWEEN THEIR ACTIONS AND THE WHOLE.

YES. THEY NEED...MOTIVATION. THEY MUST BE FORCED TO REIGNITE THE CYCLE...

YET...THEY KNOW NOTHING OF MY EXISTENCE. TO DO SO WOULD *CHANGE* THEM...

WHY LOOK ONLY TO THE FIRST?

Chapter

1

THERE ARE MANY WORLDS OPEN TO YOU, SO MANY PEOPLE...

IF YOU WERE TO STEP IN QUIETLY -- WALK AMONG THEM. THEN A SUBTLE TOUCH, TO ADD JUST A SMALL MARK OF YOUR PASSAGE -- A SIGN.

YOUR SIGN.

IMAGINE... EACH WORLD, ONE SOUL, MARKED WITH THE SIGIL. OPENED TO THE POWER.

WHY JUST ONE?

I WAS THINKING IN TERMS OF EFFICIENCY. THE NUMBER IS UNIMPORTANT. A SMALL NUMBER MAKES FOR A CLEAR BURDEN ON EACH; TOO MANY, AND THEY LET SOMEONE ELSE DO THE WORK.

AS WE HAVE ALREADY SEEN WITH THE FIRST. STILL...

COME...

WHERE ARE WE?

ON THE EDGES OF THE BLEAK ZONE. THE VERY SPOT WHERE IT ALL SEEMS TO DIE AWAY. THIS WORLD ITSELF IS A THING OF RARE BEAUTY RAVAGED BY THE CHANGES OF TIME, A PEARL DELICATELY POISED ON THE EDGE OF AN ABYSS.

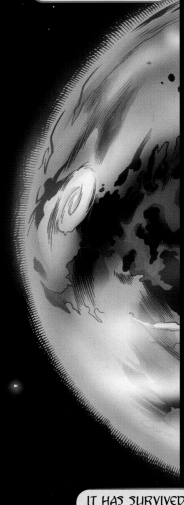

IT HAS SURVIVED ONE CATACLYSM AND ITS PEOPLE THRIVE IN THE RESULTING SKY CITIES, MANAGING A TENDER BALANCE BETWEEN THE RESOURCES AVAILABLE TO THEM AND THEIR OWN DESIRE TO POSSESS MORE.

A SINGLE SIGIL-BEARER WOULD DISRUPT THAT BALANCE. *TWO* WOULD PRESERVE THE TENSION...

TWO SIBLINGS, THIS TIME... I think...

WHAT WILL I tell them, these... *SIGIL-BEARERS*?

GIVE THEM NO WARNING, NO DIRECTION; LET THEIR ACTIONS DICTATE THE FLARE OF THE SIGIL.

THIS WILL REENERGIZE YOUR WARRIORS, BRING THEM BACK TO THEIR PURPOSE. HAVE THEM FIGHT OFF THE CHILL OF THEIR CURRENT ENNUI.

You mean CROSS-GENERATION.

YES, POWER FROM CONFLICT. ENERGY CREATING ENERGY.

AS THE NEW ONES WORK TOWARD THEIR OWN DEFINITION, THEY SERVE YOUR NEEDS.

I TELL YOU, YOU COULD START A NEW CHAIN OF CREATION TO STOKE THE COOLING FIRES OF THE WHOLE.

I FEEL IT GROWING WARMER ALREADY.

You can tell when **some** things are about to happen --

-- you can **feel** it.

Others slip by.

You just don't realize things are about to change.

Forever.

I wish I'd had some warning that day...

Hmmm... THERE'S THREE MORE SHIPS THAN USUAL.

CADADOR ALWAYS WINS IN TRADE, SEPHIE. NO MATTER WHAT IT TAKES.

JAD...

YOU *KNOW* ILAHN IS MY UNCLE...

DON'T PUT SEPHIE IN AN AWKWARD SPOT, SON.

STU -- YOU SEE THAT WOBBLE?

THOSE SHIPS HAVE BEEN MODIFIED FROM THEIR ORIGINAL FLOAT PATTERNS.

SLOPPY WORK. NOT OURS.

OF COURSE NOT! NO SHIP LEAVES MERIDIAN UNTIL IT PASSES FATHER'S FIRST RULE: *"MAKE IT PERFECT TO THE EYE AND SOUND TO THE TOUCH."*

CAN'T YOU JUST HEAR HIM SAYING--

WHOOPS!

SEE YOU AT THE RECEPTION!

IS HE HERE YET, MIRA?

RIGHT OUTSIDE.

MY LORD MINISTER...!

...PRESENTING **ILAHN**, MINISTER OF CADADOR!

STOP BARKING LIKE AN OVER-ZEALOUS HERALD, REGOR. THEY KNOW WHO I AM.

ILAHN! HOW FARES THE LAND OF CADADOR?

TUROS... MY ARM.

FORGIVE ME MY EXUBERANCE, ILAHN -- MY PRIDE IS OVERFLOWING!

JUST LOOK AT OUR SEPHIE TODAY!

GREETINGS, UNCLE.

COME -- LET US STEAL A LITTLE TIME ALONE BEFORE I LOSE YOU TO TABLE TALK!

Ah... *QUAINT* AS EVER.

TUROS... I'LL NEVER UNDERSTAND... MERIDIAN IS WEALTHY ENOUGH...

WHY CAN'T YOU RAZE THESE HOVELS AND BUILD SOMETHING MAGNIFICENT?

NOT EVERYONE HAS A TASTE FOR GILT AND ORNAMENT, ILAHN. THERE'S BEAUTY IN SIMPLICITY --

HAVE YOU FORGOTTEN THE VIEW FROM THE MOUNTAINS?

I'VE BECOME A CIVILIZED MAN, BROTHER -- ROCKS AND DIRT ARE FOR CHILDREN AND PEASANTS.

I APPRECIATE THE ART OF BRILLIANT MINDS, NOT MINDLESS NATURE.

WE MUST AGREE TO DISAGREE, THEN, ILAHN. TO YOUR HEALTH.

AND YOURS. I'VE HEARD YOU ARE... UNWELL?

I'VE KEPT IT QUIET. MY PHYSICIANS CAN'T FIND A CAUSE.

IN HONESTY, BROTHER -- I'M AFRAID, BUT I'M NOT WILLING TO SEND MY ASHES TO THE WIND JUST YET.

GIVEN YOUR CONCERNS, PERHAPS YOU'LL RECONSIDER MY OFFER TO COMBINE MERIDIAN AND CADADOR?

As it was, Papa was weak.

When it happened...

...whatever it was that did happen...

GYAAUGH!

...it was just too much.

AAAK--

TUROS? THAT CREATURE -- WHAT HAS IT DONE?!

TUROS?

PAPA?

MINISTER ILAHN! WHAT'S WRONG? IS IT THE --

NOTHING, YOU FOOL! JUST SWALLOWED SOME WINE WRONG. HELP HIM!

HELP HIM!

UNGH...

PAPA!!

SEPHIE... THE LIGHT...

PAPA, PLEASE DON'T...

As Papa slipped away, I seemed to follow him until all that was left was us... and there was nothing I could do to save him...

I felt so awful that I thought I'd die too.

Then something touched me...

...there was a BLINDING light.

It exploded right at me...

...then it flowed through me. I was filled with its warmth... suddenly, I felt protected.

I woke up realizing I was, somehow, safe.

SEPHIE! AM I TOO LATE?!

KRAAAK

YOU THERE! GET AWAY FROM HER!

BUT--

DON'T SPEAK! NO EXCUSES!

UNCLE ILAHN!

NOOOO!

YOU KILLED HIM...

ARE YOU ALL RIGHT, CHILD?

DID HE HARM YOU?

NO...

UNCLE ILAHN... I KNOW HIM...

THAT'S REGOR.

HE'S PAPA'S STEWARD.

WHY WOULD HE...

HOW COULD..?

HE TRIED TO KILL YOU BECAUSE HE WAS HIRED TO DO SO.

YOU ARE IN DANGER IF YOU STAY IN MERIDIAN.

I wish I'd thought to look back, to see everything one more time the way it was...

...but in my memories, it's still beautiful.

HURRY!

GUARDS!

SEE THAT SHE IS MADE COMFORTABLE AND SECURE ABOARD THE SHIP. I'LL BE ALONG SOON.

AND WHAT OF YOUR EARLIER ORDERS, LORD MINISTER?

WAIT UNTIL MORNING. WHEN THE FIRE BURNS DOWN... DO IT THEN.

HASTIAN -- STILL NO SIGN OF SEPHIE?

NO, MA'AM.

SUCH A WONDERFUL PLACE. WHAT A PITY.

WE'VE BEEN THROUGH THE ENTIRE PLACE.

SHE MIGHT BE OUT COLD SOMEWHERE, BUT NO ONE'S SEEN HER.

DID SEPHIE GET BURNED, HASTIAN?

SEPHIE WASN'T IN THE FIRE, JORGY...

WE DON'T KNOW WHERE SHE WENT, BUT SHE'S SAFE.

NO TUROS, NO SEPHIE... NO HOUSE ON THE HILL...

IT'S LIKE THE HEART'S BEEN TORN FROM MERIDIAN.

When CrossGen launched in May 2000, the goal was to debut with a splash. An initial release of four monthly titles seemed to be the right number, but asking fans to buy four comics to get a taste of a brand new universe of stories was asking a lot.

Hence, *CrossGen Chronicles* #1 offered an opportunity to sample the characters, worlds and stories surrounding *Mystic, Sigil, Scion,* and *Meridian*. The issue featured five-page vignettes respectively showcasing each lead character and storyline. The trick was placing them all within the context of one story, so the choice was made to use the god-like beings of the CrossGen Universe, the first, as a framing device.

It also was decided that the five-page interludes would present the characters just after they'd been granted their sigils, allowing an exploration of how they reacted to those sigils. As far as the timeline was concerned, the sequences would fit between issues #1 and #2 of the individual series. Once the #1 issues hit the stands, perceptive readers would be able to fit together the chronology. Leaving a trail of clues for clever readers to follow would become a CrossGen hallmark.

In *Meridian*, Sephie readies for her first night in a strange city without the comforting presence of the friends and family she's always known. Still in shock from witnessing her father's death and surviving an attempt on her own life, she's in the hands of the heartless uncle she does not yet know is behind her father's (his own brother's!) death and is about to discover yet another surprise related to their receiving their sigils.

Here it is, presented "in sequence" for the first time. ☙

Chapter 1.5

SO MUCH HAS CHANGED JUST IN ONE DAY I HARDLY RECOGNIZE MYSELF ANYMORE. EVERYTHING'S NEW...

...AND STRANGE.

WHATEVER IT IS WON'T EVEN COME OFF.

WHY CAN'T THE WORLD BE THE WAY IT USED TO—

AAH!

SEPHIE...

...WE SHOULD TALK.

UNCLE ILAHN! I... I DIDN'T HEAR YOU COME IN.

I HAVEN'T HAD THE CHANCE TO THANK YOU FOR... BRINGING ME TO YOUR ESTATE.

OF COURSE. WE'LL TOUR CADADOR PROPER TOMORROW.

SEPHIE, I NEED TO SHOW YOU SOMETHING.

WE'VE BOTH BEE MARKED

YOU AS WELL? DO YOU HAVE ANY IDEA WHAT THEY MEAN?

THEY'RE MARKS OF GREATNESS. OF POWER.

BUT IT'S NOT YET SAFE TO REVEAL OU SELVES. YOUR LIFE N DEPEND UPON KEEPI YOUR GIFT A SECRE

THIS IS FO YOU

THANK YOU, IT'S... PRETTY.

THE SORT OF THING YOUR MOTHER WOULD'VE WORN, I THINK. I WANT YOU TO USE IT TO *HIDE* THE MARK YOU BEAR.

IF PEOPLE KNEW WHAT WE COULD DO...

...WELL, IT'S JUST BETTER THEY *DON'T*.

REMEMBER, SEPHIE, OUR SECRET. A *FAMILY* SECRET.

I UNDERSTAND, UNCLE ILAHN.

GOOD NIGHT.

37

Chapter 2

"I wanted to write the kind of comic book I had *really* wanted to read when I was 10...so all the stops were pulled out and I'm creating my childhood fantasy."

– *Barbara Kesel*

Girls On The Side

Sephie, Minister of Meridian, looks pretty good for her age.

Oh, on the surface, she's a teen-age girl with one foot planted firmly in adolescence and the other wedged in the doorway of her adulthood, but she's actually many years older than her youthful innocence suggests.

She was born in the mind of a young Barbara Kesel, whose own youthful innocence was forcing her to question why all the girl heroes she saw in comic books, movies, and television were so useless.

"I grew up watching the *Superman* TV show and then the *Aquaman* animated Saturday-morning show, but it wasn't until I had been reading comics for a while that I noticed I wasn't seeing *me* in there," Barbara recalled. "The guy heroes grew up, took charge, and fought their own battles. Yet the girl heroes screwed up, waited for orders, or pretty much kept losing their powers. Superman and Batman led the Justice League, but Wonder Woman – this immortal Amazon who had powers rivaling Superman's – was the secretary of the Justice League. It just made me wonder why she put up with being treated like that."

And it wasn't any different when Barbara watched movies or television shows or the news.

"You could watch *Star Trek* to get a sense of heroes, but the gals were only on the radio, not in the captain's chair, or being nurses, not doctors," she said. "The space program was in full force, but only men were astronauts, which gave me a strong sense of my second-class position in the world. At the same time, though, within my peer group there didn't seem to be too many differences in or limits on what we could do. In the background, the women's movement, civil rights marches, Vietnam, and other events I was only barely

> **"Now we have introduced Sephie to the world. And Sephie never stops being a girl...but nothing stops her. In a nutshell, that's what makes her the most dynamic girl hero in comics today."**

aware of were changing the world, so even though the message existed that my gender would 'hold me back,' it also seemed like the world that would exist when I grew up would be very different."

After digesting all of that data and socialization, the grown-up Barbara began transferring all she had learned and all that disappointed her about the lack of strong female role models into the one medium she truly loved: comic books.

"I wanted to write the kind of comic book I had *really* wanted to read when I was 10," Barbara said. "So when I started writing my own, I added in some 'girl-friendly' bits while remaining aware that the primary audience for this medium is still guys. In the case of *Meridian*, though, we wanted to *target* girls, so all the stops were pulled out and I'm creating my childhood fantasy."

And that was the genesis of Sephie. Barbara knew what kind of girl hero she wanted, but she didn't quite have the right venue. At DC Comics, as a professional writer and editor, she wrote stories for characters like Batgirl and Supergirl, but they all had decades of superficial baggage to drag them down. They were more stereotype than character, and she was looking for something more: a girl with spunk. Guts. Personality. Somebody caught in that twilight zone between kid and grown-up. Somebody *fun*.

"I wanted to see comics where the girls did what I'd do in my childhood dreams, and it's kinda nice to be in a position all grown up where I can do that now," Barbara beamed. "Now we have introduced Sephie to the world. And Sephie never stops being a girl...but *nothing* stops her. In a nutshell, that's what makes her the most dynamic girl hero in comics today. My 10-year-old self is proud."

Cadador, on the other hand...

...wore peace like a beautiful robe -- hiding its weapons inside the folds.

DID YOU HEAR? CADADORIAN TROOPS

INVASION FORCE

MERIDIAN'S BEEN TAKEN OVER!

WE'RE INVADING MERIDIAN?

WHAT? ARE THEY TALKING ABOUT *MERIDIAN?*

STREET TALK. DON'T TROUBLE YOURSELF WITH RUMORS, SEPHIE.

OVER A THOUSAND TROOPERS

AT LAST! MORE ROOM

BURNED TO THE GROUND

BUT IF SOMETHING HAS HAPPENED...!

FIVE SHIPLOADS OF MEN

ABOUT TIME WE SOLVED THE PROBLEM

PAPA ALWAYS SAID I HAVE A RESPONSIBILITY TO MERIDIAN FIRST!

I *HAVE* TO GO *HOME.*

HOME? RESP--

YOU *DO* HAVE A RESPONSIBILITY TO MERIDIAN. TO STAY HERE IN CADADOR.

TO *LEARN.* TO *GROW.* TO BECOME A *GREAT* MINISTER.

IF YOU GO HOME NOW, YOU PUT MERIDIAN IN THE HANDS OF AN AMATEUR...

...A MINISTER UNSCHOOLED IN THE TRICKS OF TRADE...

IS THAT THE *RESPONSIBLE* THING TO DO?

NO.

YOU'RE LEARNING ALREADY. GOOD GIRL.

HERE'S WHAT WILL HAPPEN.

YOU REMAIN MINISTER IN EXILE...

I JUST DON'T UNDERSTAND WHY ANYONE WOULD WANT TO HURT *ME...*

...WE PLACE A REGENT TO MAINTAIN ORDER AND PRODUCTION.

AND FERRET OUT TRAITORS -- YOUR WOULD-BE ASSASSIN MAY NOT HAVE ACTED ALONE!

SEPHIE! THE MINUTE YOUR FATHER DIED, *YOU* BECAME A *TARGET!*

DO YOU HAVE ANY IDEA HOW MUCH WEALTH MERIDIAN REPRESENTS?

YOU INHERIT, BUT UNLESS YOU HAVE THE POWER BASE TO ASSERT YOUR RULE...

...THERE ARE ALWAYS THOSE WHO WOULD TAKE IT AWAY FROM YOU...BY ANY MEANS.

AND UNTIL WE DETERMINE WHO LED THAT ATTACK ON YOUR LIFE...

...YOU'RE SAFER *HERE.*

It seemed like my whole life was washing away, fading into the gray of Cadador...

...but it was only m childhood ending...

...Only a day before I was racing through Meridian, thinking about Jad....

HFF HFF

THERE! ON THE ROOF!

DON'T LOSE THIS ONE! WE NEED TO KNOW HOW SO MANY MERIDIANITES KEEP *DISAPPEARING!*

KLAK KLAK KLAK KLAK

SKREECK

SEPHIE...

"...IT'S NOT LIKE THERE'S ANY SHADOWS TO HIDE IN!"

...TO GUARANTEE MERIDIAN AS PROSPEROUS AND SUCCESSFUL A FUTURE AS CADADOR!

STRONG SPEECH FROM THE MOUTH OF A MAN WHO WOULD PLANT THE KISS OF DEATH ON HIS OWN BROTHER'S LIPS!

SHE... KNOWS?

WHO ARE YOU, CREATURE?

I AM THE ONE WHO SEES WHAT IS TO COME...

...TWO SIDES IN OPPOSITION, NEVER TO TOUCH...

...I SEE YOUR SIGIL, EVEN THOUGH YOU HIDE ITS OUTER ASPECT...

YOU... SEE--?

I-- I--

BOSCAU! HAVE THAT...WOMAN BROUGHT TO MY STUDY.

HAVE HER CLEANED FIRST.

FAREWELL, MY FRIENDS! OUR PLAN IS IN MOTION, AND I'M OFF TO HOME!

NO.

AAAH!

WHAM

FINE!

THEY CAN'T STOP ME LIKE THIS!

THEY *CAN'T* STOP ME...

ISRE, KIKKAH -- I NEITHER WANT NOR DESIRE YOUR ASSISTANCE ANYMORE TONIGHT...

...I WISH TO BE ALONE WITH MY OWN THOUGHTS...

...*YOU ARE DISMISSED.*

HMPFH! AS YOU WISH! GOOD NIGHT --

"--I HAVE *OTHER* DUTIES TO ATTEND TO, ANYWAY!"

NOK NOK

ENTER!

THE MINISTER OF CADADOR REQUESTED AN AUDIENCE WITH THIS... WOMAN?

I DID. SEE HER IN.

WE... DID OUR BEST, BUT...

YOU WISHED THEM TO CHANGE ME, BUT I WILL NOT BE CHANGED. I AM WHAT I CHOSE TO BE.

YOU HAVE CHANGED.

Hmmm, I SEE -- YOU CALLED HER *HEARTSTEALER,* THEN -- *SILENCE!*

PLEASE EXCUSE US.

LEAVE!

WHO ARE YOU...

Ilahn rules Cadador, but won't live on its land. He has his own island tethered at its side.

He doesn't really KNOW his city...

I know every inch of Meridian.

All around me, busy people filled the night with conversation, not shy about sharing their concerns... never noticing me.

Without the pronouncement of my title, I was invisible, just passing by like a ghost.

A ghost HEARING horrors, not causing them...

...I heard how these people, the lowsiders, weren't treated as well as those above...

How the people who lived below the horizon were thought of as less important than others of their SAME CITY...

How these people HATED my uncle for reinforcing the divisions of class.

And all the things they said he did...

A good Minister, they all said...

...but not a good man.

I always knew he wasn't as good a man as my father, but I hadn't had a chance to NOTICE what I'd been seeing...

Uncle Ilahn WASN'T a good man...

...and now he was in control of Meridian...

Oh, PAPA, I KNOW WHAT YOU'D SAY...

"LIFE HAS TOSSED YOU A TWIST -- TRY TO BEND WITH IT."

BUT THIS PLACE...

...IT JUST ISN'T... HOME.

Chapter 3

"[Sephie] is good-natured and kind, with a little rebel hidden inside, but has never faced any great crises in her life. Then we put her through incredible horror."

– Barbara Kesel

Sephie – A Different Kind of Hero

Before a single announcement was made about the launch of CrossGen's new line of comics, there was a feeling in the studio that *Meridian* was going to be a very different comic book story.

It wasn't simply going to be different from the other CrossGen titles, but it was going to be different from any other comic book on the market. The hero was a girl, but not just any girl – a *normal* girl. In comics, that's unheard of.

To be a traditional comic book female, you have to be Amazonian in proportions, wear impossibly tight Spandex, and remain a secondary character for the length of your existence. Traditionally, comic books about girls – unless they are comics that use the female lead character as a sex object – don't sell well.

So not only would *Meridian* feature a girl hero, but it would feature a girl hero who wasn't a supermodel-type who used sex appeal or a super-physique to save the day. She would be a normal teenager thrown into extraordinary circumstances who, initially, would survive on her wits, her gumption, and the power of an unusual imprint on her forehead, the Sigil.

And she would have to grow up very, very fast.

"With Sephie, I tried to create a complete character – plusses and minuses, virtues

and vices, and we were also trying to walk that very fine line between childhood and adulthood," said *Meridian* writer Barbara Kesel. "She's crossed the midpoint, but one foot is still dragging behind, so she can be the petulant child who whines when she isn't let out of her room in Cadador, or the wily adventurer who gets herself out on the town to explore, as well as the budding Minister who knows how to cull the lesson from what she learns when out exploring.

"With Sephie, I tried to create a complete character – plusses and minuses, virtues and vices, and we were also trying to walk that very fine line between childhood and adulthood."

She's spunky but fearful – still a little naïve about the world at large."

Visually, art director Brandon Peterson and penciler Joshua Middleton worked to give Sephie the appearance of the archetypal teenager, with just a hint of spirit.

"Sephie is not a standard super-heroine in comics in that she has an adolescent body type rather than the more mature body types we

see in comics today," Brandon said. "Her movement and gesture is of an adolescent girl and not a mature woman. We try to keep a spirit of optimism and cheeriness about her, too, and her appearance reflects that. Her bright sunny hair, her fashion sense, and the way she carries herself all reflect subtle naïveté, the optimistic innocence of youth."

And from that visual starting point, the character of Sephie is propelled into an odyssey that will erase everything she knows and loves in her life and replace those comforts with seemingly insurmountable challenges.

"We start out with an independent but sheltered girl living in a protected environment with a very limited view of what exists beyond her immediate world," Barbara explained. "She knows much more than she has experienced, but she hasn't had an opportunity to put that knowledge to use. She is good-natured and kind, with a little rebel hidden inside, but has never faced any great crises in her life. Then we put her through incredible horror. She is in the process of discovering she has the resources to survive and emerge thriving on the other side of this trauma better off than when she started. She is forced to grow up physically, emotionally, culturally, and politically."

...or if he'd been forgotten in the panic when the soldiers from Cadador invaded.

So, not knowing, I did what I could.

GOODBYE, PAPA.

GOOD JOURNEY.

AAIEEE!

YES, ISRE?

CHILD, HAVE YOU LOST YOUR MIND? COME DOWN FROM THERE!

MINISTER ILAHN REQUESTS YOUR PRESENCE...

WHAT'S WRONG? YOUR ESCAPE WENT PERFECTLY, AND THAT *RESCUE*...

NOTHING'S WRONG.

YOU THINK *SEPHIE* SAW THAT?

SO... JUST WHERE *IS* SHE?

WE DON'T KNOW, JAD.

WE THINK SHE MAY HAVE GONE WITH ILAHN.

WHA--?

TO CADADOR?

SHE'D NEVER-- MIRA, I'VE GOT TO GO GET HER BACK!

JAD, *NO!*

WE JUST KEPT YOU OUT OF THE HANDS OF THE CADADORIAN SOLDIERS! DON'T GO RUSHING BACK IN!

DON'T YOU TELL ME WHAT TO DO! YOU'RE NOT MY MOTHER!

JAD!

FEABIE...

MORE MYSTERIES!

DAMN YOU, MUSE...

...WE'VE BEEN AT THIS FOR TOO MANY HOURS NOW.

YOU GIVE ME OBSCURITIES AND HINTS WHEN I'M ASKING FOR INFORMATION!

THE EYES OF THE MUSE OF GIATAN SEE MANY THINGS. THE EYES OF THE MINISTER OF CADADOR ARE CLOUDED WITH NEED...

YES, I NEED!

I NEED TO KNOW IF THIS ABILITY IS A FUNCTION OF MY OWN NATURE...

...OR IF THE POWER I NOW POSSESS IS DUPLICATED IN MY NIECE!

UNCLE ILAHN?

THEY SAID...

COVER YOURSELF!

YOU SEE THE ANSWER, BUT YOU DO NOT KNOW IT...

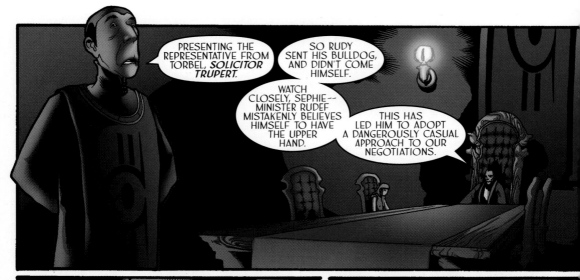

PRESENTING THE REPRESENTATIVE FROM TORBEL, *SOLICITOR TRUPERT.*

SO RUDY SENT HIS BULLDOG, AND DIDN'T COME HIMSELF.

WATCH CLOSELY, SEPHIE-- MINISTER RUDEF MISTAKENLY BELIEVES HIMSELF TO HAVE THE UPPER HAND.

THIS HAS LED HIM TO ADOPT A DANGEROUSLY CASUAL APPROACH TO OUR NEGOTIATIONS.

MINISTER ILAHN! MINISTER RUDEF SENDS GREETINGS FROM TORBEL.

IT'S PAST TIME TO RENEW OUR ORE SUPPLY AGREEMENT.

SINCE WE DIDN'T RECEIVE A COURIER FROM CADADOR AND OUR SUPPLY IS RUNNING SHORT, HE SENT ME TO FINALIZE THE DEAL.

THERE'S A SMALL PROBLEM, I'M AFRAID.

TORBEL HAS *CHEATED* CADADOR.

YOU HAVE DELIVERED ORE VATS THAT I KNOW TO BE INFERIOR TO THOSE OF YOUR NEWEST PRODUCTION RUN.

CHEATED?

THERE'S NO CHEAT INVOLVED!

WE CONTACTED YOU, ILAHN. YOU WERE MADE AWARE THAT OUR MASTER IRONWORKERS HAD DESIGNED NEW, MORE EFFICIENT AND MORE EXPENSIVE ORE VATS!

YOU DIDN'T WANT TO PAY MORE, SO WE SUPPLIED VATS OF THE CONTRACTED STYLE AT THE CONTRACTED PRICE!

BUT I HAVE REVIEWED OUR CONTRACT. IT SPECIFIES THAT CADADOR WILL RECEIVE THE *FINEST AVAILABLE*.

YOU DRAFTED AND SIGNED AN AGREEMENT WITH THAT PROVISION INCLUDED.

THEREFORE, YOU SHOULD HAVE AUTOMATICALLY SHIPPED THE BETTER VATS.

THAT'S SALES PUFFERY, ILAHN!

THAT LANGUAGE ISN'T IN THE BODY OF THE CONTRACT -- I WON'T LET YOU PLAY A GAME OF WEASEL WORDS HERE!

DAMN YOU, MAN -- YOU'RE WITHHOLDING ORE, PUTTING TORBEL IN JEOPARDY OVER A CASUAL PHRASE!

I'M NOT WITHHOLDING ORE. WE HAVE NO CURRENT CONTRACT FOR SUPPLY.

AND I DON'T MAKE *NEW* BUSINESS WITH THOSE WHO DO NOT KEEP THEIR WORD.

WE'RE FINISHED HERE. SEE THE MAN TO THE DOOR, BOSCAU.

BUT--

BUT--

ILAHN, DO YOU KNOW WHAT YOU'RE DOING?

TORBEL IS *MASSIVE*.

WITHOUT THAT ORE TO KEEP US ALOFT, TORBEL WILL *FALL!*

MINISTER ILAHN HAS CONCLUDED YOUR MEETING, SIR.

When Father did business, no one left the table until both sides were satisfied.

He wouldn't leave another city in danger.

Of course, we built ships on Meridian. No one would die if you refused to sell them a ship.

NOW, SEPHIE... WHAT DID YOU LEARN HERE?

It hurt me to realize Uncle Ilahn was willing to make good on his threat...

...all because of their attitude at the table...

...and a few miswritten words.

THAT PEOPLE SHOULD ALWAYS MAKE SURE THEY KEEP TO THE LETTER OF AN AGREEMENT, NOT JUST ITS INTENT.

PERCEPTION OF INTENT.

IF INTENT IS NOT CLEARLY OUTLINED IN THE LANGUAGE OF A CONTRACT, IT CANNOT BE USED AS AN EXCUSE FOR NON-PERFORMANCE OF SPECIFIED DUTIES.

BUT I HEARD...

A LOT OF PEOPLE IN CADADOR DON'T FAVOR A HOSTILE RELATIONSHIP WITH OTHER CITES.

WHERE DID YOU HEAR THAT?

Ah... AROUND.

WOULD YOU REALLY LET TORBEL FALL?

ONLY IF NECESSARY...

"...SOMETIMES ENFORCEMENT OF NEGATIVE CONSEQUENCES IS NECESSARY FOR THE FUTURE OF A BUSINESS RELATIONSHIP."

KEEP MOVING!

AFTER THREE MORE TURNS OF THE TRAIL THERE'S A HUT. GO BEHIND, NOT IN--

MERILY'S GIRLS WILL GUIDE YOU DOWN TO THE CENTER ROAD TO BEACON NOTCH AND THE OTHERS.

WE'RE NEARLY THE LAST. THE MINISTER'S STAFF AND THE COUNCIL ARE ON THEIR WAY.

WHAT ABOUT YOU, JON?

I'LL BE ALONG SOON.

THOSE CADAPORIAN SOLDIERS DON'T KNOW THE HILLS OF MERIDIAN, AND I'VE GOT THEM OUT-NUMBERED...

THERE'S ONLY THREE OF THEM.

HOLD.

THAT'S STRANGE. THERE'S NO SIGN OF--

PSST!

THAT'S ONE!

GLASS JAW.

YOU'RE JUST BOYS UNDER THOSE MASKS!

YOU MAY SEE YOURSELVES AS THE MIGHTY INVADING ARMY, BUT YOU'RE JUST CHILDREN!

There was some good in Cadador's business.

Wealth made the city a great benefactor of artists.

I missed Meridian and Papa, but the pleasing result of one man's imagination made me feel a little more at home in this place that was so very...

...strange.

SO, YOU ARE BEGINNING TO SEE HIM MORE CLEARLY.

YOU SENSE THAT THE MEASURE OF YOUR FATHER'S BROTHER AS A MAN FALLS SHORT.

AAAH!

YOU EVEN BEGIN TO FEAR HIM...

I DIDN'T -- WHAT MAKES YOU SAY THAT?

I AM THE EYES.

I CANNOT HELP BUT SEE THE SECRETS.

ASK HIM, CHILD.

ASK HIM WHY HE KEEPS COLD ECHOING MEMORIES CLUTCHED INSIDE.

ASK HIM WHY THE PORTRAIT HE WEARS CLOSE TO HIS HEART BEARS YOUR MOTHER'S LIKENESS.

MY MOTHER?

I-- I'LL ASK HIM... NOW!

EX-EXCUSE ME...THANK YOU!

82

I remember being afraid that I would be so overwhelmed by Cadador's ways that I would start being one of them...

...that I would forget to NOTICE the beauty around me.

UNCLE ILAHN!

TO SCHEDULE A BANQUET FOR MYSELF AND THE OTHER MINISTERS WHERE I SHALL MAKE MY OFFICIAL ANNOUNCEMENT

UNCLE ILAHN! I HAVE TO TALK TO YOU!

NOT NOW, SEPHIE.

SEE TO THE LIST, LOROSI.

I WANT IT READY FOR MY REVIEW AND SIGNATURE TONIGHT.

YES, LORD MINISTER.

UNCLE ILAHN, IS IT TRUE?

DO YOU WEAR A PORTRAIT OF MY MOTHER?

UHP!

When I left Cadador that day...

...I not only left behind my only living relative...

...I left behind my first true enemy.

But I didn't care.

After all, I was the Daughter of Meridian...

...and I was going home.

Chapter

Meridian's True Colors

In just about every review of the issues of *Meridian* contained in this volume, the look and feel of the art has been compared to an animated feature and even Disney films.

Not only was that not a coincidence, it was all part of the plan.

"Early on, we decided that *Meridian* was going to be the title we would make the most accessible to a comics audience that is practically nonexistent – young girls," recalled CrossGen art director Brandon Peterson. "One thing we saw was that the softer *manga* style was very popular with the (already small) portion of the young female population who read comic books. We also drew from the more traditional influences of classic animated features and other girls' entertainment, leaning toward softer, more 'Disney-esque' qualities."

Barbara even lent a hand by flooding Brandon and his art team of penciler Joshua Middleton, inker Dexter Vines, and colorist Mike Atiyeh with a variety of additional classic references.

"I brought in illustrations from turn-of-the-century children's books – fairy tales, basically," Barbara said. "Plenty of examples of the old-fashioned illustrative style from the first period of time in which books were produced *for* children and *about* children. The late Victorian era first

romanticized childhood, creating books with illustrations that played up the perfection and innocence of the childhood years. Since then, children's books have matured, but most of the artistic bases for fairy-tale imagery that we have today are rooted in the imagery of Arthur Rackham, Howard Pyle, Charles and William Heath Robinson, Alexander Caldicott, Sir John Tenniel, Ivan Bilibin, Maxfield Parrish and so many others. If we were going to tell a fairy tale,

---

"If we were going to tell a fairy tale, even a more modernized one like *Meridian*, then we should have it look like one, too."

---

even a more modernized one like *Meridian*, then we should have it look like one, too."

Of immeasurable value in that quest was the palette of *Meridian* colorist Mike Atiyeh.

"The palettes used accentuate this fairy-tale quality in the drawing, and Mike Atiyeh's initial palette choices were spot-on and have been used ever since," said Brandon. "*Meridian's* artistic feel has often been compared to that of an

animated feature. I consider that to be a compliment to the very capable artists who have worked on this book. And Mike uses his colors very differently than a mainstream superhero comic book does. In those comics, the colorist generally tries to convey strong, vibrant primary and secondary colors to underscore the action taking place on the page. Mike chose a palette that was subdued and very controlled; pastels mixed with rich earth tones to create a feeling of nature as seen through the rose-colored glasses of youth."

Mike's reasoning for that choice was simple. He didn't want to use his colors to convey action. He wanted to convey *emotion*.

"Basically, I wanted to make the book *feel*. I wanted to play with mood a lot. I wanted to show feelings," Mike said. "I wanted the colors around Sephie to show happiness when we showed her with her father. I wanted to show Ilahn's mood when he first showed his true colors, so I went a bit darker, but I wanted to do it in such way that we never lost the underlying beauty of the floating city of Meridian. I tried to take this book out of comics and more into the realm of animation. I tried to take *Meridian* away from superhero comics and instead use more realistic colors from the world around us to capture the beauty that can be seen in everyday life."

I was anxious to see Meridian again.

When they said that Cadador had invaded Meridian, my mind jumped right to horror stories of war from Pre-Cataclysm days, and I pictured something bloody and awful.

I forgot that an army, like a business, comes down to just PEOPLE...

...and the people of Meridian are strong.

CONGRATULATIONS, JON TAKARTY! YOU'RE THE FIRST OF MERIDIAN'S COUNCILORS TO BE DETAINED.

KLANNG

YOU RUSTICS ARE HARD TO FIND, BUT THE OTHERS CAN'T HIDE FOR LONG...

...WE'LL BRING THEM IN SOON.

YOU MAY HAVE TAKEN THE LAND OF MERIDIAN, BUT DON'T THINK YOU'LL TAKE HER PEOPLE SO EASILY.

WE'LL SEE, OLD MAN.

KWHACK

WHAT HAPPENED TO THE PARTY I WAS LEADING UP THE HILLS?

ALREADY DOWN THE CENTER ROAD. THEY'RE HALFWAY TO BEACON NOTCH BY NOW. ONE MORE STOP AND WE'RE NEXT.

THAT'S COMFORTING.

I QUESTIONED TUROS' WISDOM WHEN HE DECIDED TO EXPAND THE MAZE, BUT IT'S CERTAINLY A BOON TO US NOW.

THERE'S AN ACCESS NEARBY?

UNDER YOUR NOSE.

ME, I'VE SPENT THE LAST DECADE MAPPING AND EXPANDING THE TUNNELS WHILE *SOME* PEOPLE FLITTED AROUND ON BOATS...

KREEEEK

...PROBABLY THE ONLY PERSON WHO KNOWS THESE PASSAGES AS WELL AS I DO IS *SEPHIE*...

...THAT GIRL'S BEEN CURIOUS AS A CAT SINCE SHE COULD WALK!

I HOPE SHE'S WELL...

Racing away from Cadador, I felt my heart leap for the first time since Papa died...

Home! Fair winds or foul, I was on my way...

...flying a ship that usually takes a crew of three, but I'd done that before.

The familiar, automatic actions left me free to think about everything that had happened.

I wasn't sure exactly how I'd stop an invasion by a whole army...

...but it had to be done.

I couldn't let Uncle Ilahn destroy Meridian.

I was Minister now. It was my job to protect...

...MERIDIAN?

Uncle Ilahn's estate...

...all my visits, and I'd never SEEN it.

I'd heard whispers of foolish construction...

...but no one ever told me he'd carved his little island into a copy of Meridian!

Maybe that's why Papa always berthed our ship on the other side?

But I ran out of time to fume...

...Cadadorian soldiers had spotted me!

VRAROOOT

I'd expected them to chase me...

...but not so soon!

ATTENTION, RUNAWAY SHIP!

PLEASE CUT YOUR SAILS AND PREPARE TO BE BOARDED!

For an instant, I nearly followed orders...

..."mind your elders"...

...before I remembered that this order came from a CADADORIAN soldier!

Jad showed me a great stunt once.

It only works with the little airships.

You have to trick the wind into forcing you down against the ship's natural buoyancy.

You shift the ballast, set the sails to catch the shear, and hold on tight!

He calls it the "Death Dive."

You have to be very confident in your shiphandling abilities...

...and you can't be afraid to see the ground...

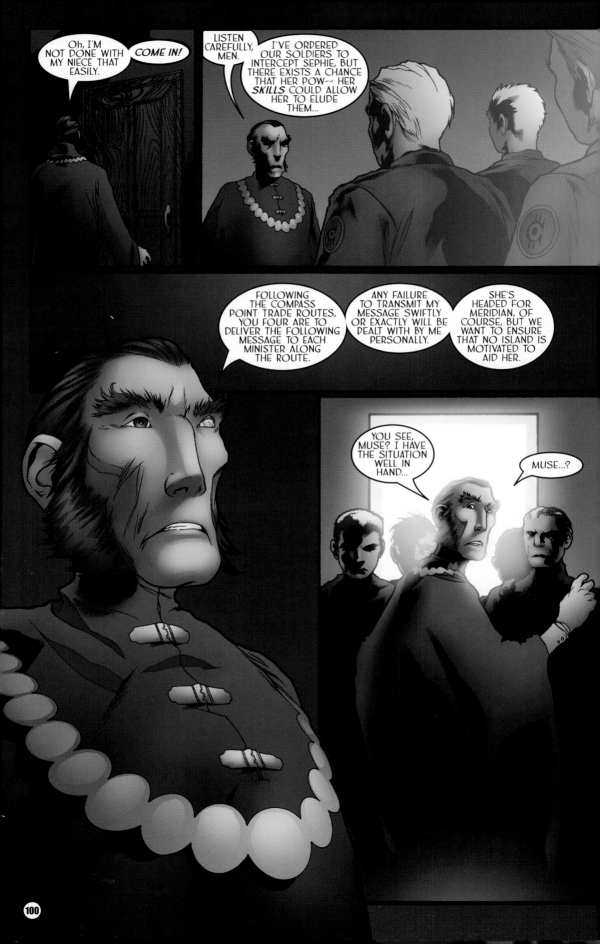

THANKS FOR YOUR HELP, NORY.

Oh, HA! LIKE TURNING A WINCH IS DANGEROUS LABOR!

I DID THE SAME FOR YOUR BOY, JON, GOING THE OTHER DIRECTION.

HE'S A FEARLESS ONE, THAT JAD.

YOU JUST RUSH BACK HERE ONCE YOU'VE GOT THE LAST ONES SO WE CAN ALL BE ON OUR WAY DOWN.

MY BARIA'S GONE AHEAD ALREADY...

TOO QUIET, JON-- AND FRISHA'S NOT IN SIGHT.

THEY'RE INSIDE.

GO BACK!

GO BACK DOWN! IT'S A TRAP!

NO, FRISHA-- --WE WON'T LEAVE YOU, GIRL!

NO ONE WHO'S AGREED TO GO GETS LEFT BEHIND!

WHOMP

KRAAK

WHUMPF

IT'S BEEN A LONG TIME, BREHN.

I NEVER THOUGHT YOU'D COME BACK...

I DIDN'T. I'M JUST HERE AS A CADADORIAN SOLDIER.

YOU'D BETTER GET GOING...

...BUT SOMEBODY'S GOT TO HIT ME OR I'LL HAVE TOO MUCH TO EXPLAIN.

HAPPY TO OBLIGE.

YOU'RE WHERE YOU BELONG NOW, BOY-- --WITH CADADOR'S MERCENARIES!

DON'T CRY FOR HIM, LISELA. THIS GOOD DEED DOESN'T REDEEM HIS TRANSGRESSIONS.

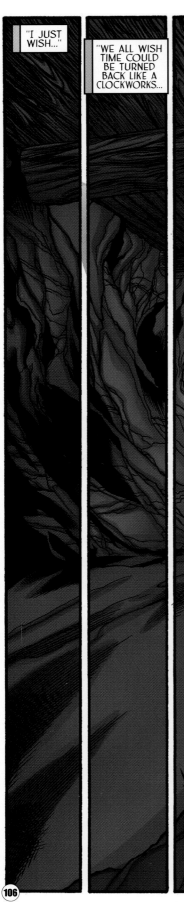

"I JUST WISH..."

"WE ALL WISH TIME COULD BE TURNED BACK LIKE A CLOCKWORKS..."

"...BUT IT ONLY MOVES FORWARD, AS MUST WE."

IS IT TRUE THIS TUNNEL LEADS UNDER *EVERY* BUILDING?

SON, BETTER THAN *THAT!*

THE TUNNELS LEAD ALL THE WAY DOWN TO BEACON POINT...

...AND ON TO *FREEDOM!*

The Cadadorian soldiers were better sailors than I expected...

...I knew I was about to be caught.

LET'S COORDINATE THE SPEARS--

--WAIT ON MY *SIGNAL!*

But no one waited.

They were all afraid somebody else would get the credit...

So too many spears were cast...

NO! THAT CRAFT'S TOO LIGHT!

LET THE LINES GO SLACK!

...from too many ships more massive than mine...

...so my ship stopped still...

...dead still...

...but I didn't.

As I tumbled, it was almost funny to watch it all twist around...

...you see, now, instead of fighting over who got the credit...

...it would be about who got the blame...

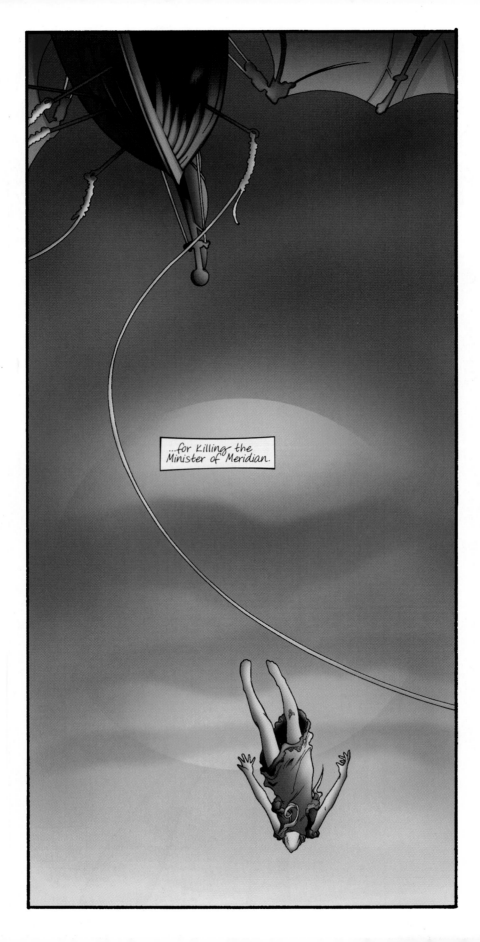

...for killing the Minister of Meridian.

Chapter 5

While Jad's only interaction with Sephie is at the beginning of this volume's story, the impact he has on Sephie's world — and hers on his — is important.

— from production notes

Extended Family Affair

Not everything in *Meridian* is made up of opposites. There are some things that Sephie and Ilahn have in common. For instance, they each have a foil. Well, sort of.

Two characters – the young Jad Takarty and the Muse of Giatan – each play pivotal roles in the lives of their respective acquaintances. Jad, a potential love interest for Sephie, reinforces that alongside being the Minister's daughter and, now, the tragic hero-to-be of Demetria, Sephie is also a teen-age girl. For Ilahn, the Muse is a character who possesses a mysterious hold on the Minister of Cadador, feeding him inspiration at times, instigation at other times. While Jad's only interaction with Sephie is at the beginning of this volume's story, the impact he has on Sephie's world – and hers on his – is important.

Presented here for the first time in print are *Meridian* writer Barbara Kesel's character design notes for these two pivotal characters, with additional comments from CrossGen's art director Brandon Peterson.

"**The Muse of Giatan –** *She appeared on the streets of Cadador after Ilahn gained his sigil. She recognized its shape, surprising him, and he has kept her by him as his adviser ever since. Others may wonder what hold this strange crone has on the leader of the most powerful state on this world, but he knows that she has knowledge that comes from beyond. She parcels out hints in*

exchange for room and board but never tells enough to keep Ilahn satisfied. She seems almost formless until she speaks, at which time her orange eyes light up, her hands weave out the shape of the 'prophecy' she tells, and she seems to take up more space than when she is quiet."

"The Muse was a bit of a challenge in that we wanted to convey power, but in a non-threatening way," Brandon explained. "She is a mysterious advisor to Ilahn but is not frightening to him. She is this old woman who

---

> ## "The Muse was a bit of a challenge in that we wanted to convey power, but in a non-threatening way."

---

sees into the future and has the power of knowledge but is physically unintimidating. We made her shriveled and hunched to convey this quality even more. Ilahn has no equals in his mind and definitely no superiors, so it was important for the Muse's physicality to reflect no visible threat to Ilahn."

"**Jad Takarty –** *Jon's son, Jad has been Sephie's best friend since they were both children. He's also an accomplished airship sailor and has a big crush on Sephie (and she on him), although he feels the Minister's daughter is 'above*

his station.' Sephie loves to spend time with her 'big brother,' although she no longer thinks of him that way. Jad is 17, in his athletic prime, and dressed in the rugged, coarse breeches and shirt look we've established for the sailors."

"For Jad, Sephie's love interest, we knew we wanted to make him her contemporary," Brandon said. "He is of similar age as and possesses similar spirit to Sephie and can be likened to Leo DiCaprio with his open, flowing clothing and his slightly mussed hair and stereotypical dimples."

For many of the characters in *Meridian*, the art team decided to style them less as comic book characters and more as characters one would see in an animated feature or television series. The formula that is more artistically prevalent in these venues is to go for something more stereotypical in nature to make it easier for a younger audience to identify the characters and tell them apart. The challenge in adopting that look is to refrain from going overboard.

"One of our goals was to keep from alienating the traditional comic audience by not taking the stereotypes to their fullest extent," Brandon said. "I think Josh Middleton and [later] Steve McNiven have been very successful in this aspect. The artwork is uncluttered, elegant, with a simplicity of line that is neither threatening nor condescending." 🔁

TORBEL, THE IRONWORKERS' CITY.

MINISTER ILAHN OF CADADOR SENDS HIS REGARDS AND THIS MESSAGE TO THE MINISTER OF TORBEL:

"SEPHIE, THE MINISTER OF MERIDIAN--"

VYLUND, WHERE LAWYERS ARE TAUGHT AND TESTED.

"-- HAS FLED MINISTER ILAHN'S CITY IN A FIT OF GRIEF.

"SHE IS YOUNG, AND HAS SUFFERED UNPRECEDENTED TRAGEDY..."

RING CITY, HOME OF BOOKBINDERS.

"...SO IS LIKELY HEADED HOME TO MERIDIAN.

"BUT TO MY FELLOW MINISTERS AND CLOSEST NEIGHBORS MAY I MAKE THIS SUGGESTION..."

NESCOAN, CITY OF CARRIAGEMAKERS.

"...RECEIVE HER COURTEOUSLY SHOULD SHE COME TO YOU.

"AND SEND A MESSENGER TO CADADOR IMMEDIATELY.

"SO I MAY ARRANGE FOR HER RETURN TO MY CARE."

113

In Meridian, the first story all children know is the tale about the monster called the Edge.

"Stay AWAY from the Edge."

"Children DIE at the Edge."

"You weren't playing near the EDGE?"

Every so often, a child is taken by the monster.

When we get older, we realize that although the Edge is real...

...the monster is just a tale to frighten children away from danger.

But although the monster doesn't exist...

...you suddenly understand the true danger of the edge...

...and you realize what happened to those children.

That's when the fear becomes REAL.

Then you grow up, and the Edge becomes just one more ordinary danger.

You don't think about the monster anymore.

At least, I didn't.

Until now.

The Monster had me.

I was going to join those lost children...

...so why wasn't I afraid?

MINISTER ILAHN?

HE'S STILL ASLEEP.

THE MINISTER WAS UP ALL LAST NIGHT INTERROGATING THAT GROTESQUE WOMAN.

THEN THAT WRETCHED NIECE OF HIS FLED...

...HE'S BEEN THROUGH ENOUGH FOR ONE DAY.

SEPHIE'S TRAGEDY WON'T CHANGE BEFORE MORNING.

BEST TO WAIT AND GIVE HIM THE NEWS ABOUT HER DEATH WHEN HE'S RESTED.

AYE. WE NEEDN'T ADD PAIN TO PAIN NOW.

Oh? IS IT HIS PAIN OR YOURS THAT CONCERNS YOU?

Uh...

...DAD?

DAD?

I--

--I'M SO SORRY, JAD--

-- BUT THERE JUST HADN'T BEEN A GOOD TIME TO TELL YOU...

Uh... OKAY.

BUT... YOU JUST *HAVEN'T*... NOT SINCE MOM...

YOUR MOTHER WOULDN'T BEGRUDGE ME A SECOND CHANCE.

I *KNOW*, DAD!

IT'S NOT THAT!

DID I HAVE TO FIND OUT *AFTER* EVERYBODY ELSE?

MIRA, *YOU* COULD HAVE LET ME KNOW...

BUT, JAD, YOU SAID IT YOURSELF...

...I'M NOT YOUR MOTHER.

ILAHN'S CASTLE...

...THE PRIDE OF CADADOR...

...MY NEW HOME.

NOK NOK

YESSSS?

GOOD MORNING!

I'D LIKE TO ARRANGE AN APPOINTMENT WITH MINISTER ILAHN.

YOU ARE CLEARLY THE MAJOR DOMO OF HIS ESTATE.

I'M CERTAIN *YOU* COULD ARRANGE IT.

THERE ARE PROTOCOLS...

...WHICH ARE DESIGNED TO CONTROL THOSE WHO MINDLESSLY TAKE DIRECTION...

...NOT FOR INDEPENDENT THINKERS LIKE US.

CERTAINLY YOU COULD JUST SLIP ME IN ON HIS AGENDA...

Hmmmm....

COME BACK THIS AFTERNOON. I'LL SEE WHAT'S AVAILABLE.

LOROSI!

SSHHHH KLEK

YES, MY MINISTER?

SEND IN THE CAPTAIN.

I'M ANXIOUS TO HEAR WHAT CAPTAIN PATGIEN HAS TO SAY ABOUT WHY MY NIECE HAS NOT BEEN RETURNED TO ME.

YES, MY MINISTER.

STORM CLOUDS ON THE HORIZON.

MINISTER ILAHN.

WELCOME, CAPTAIN PATGIEN! COME IN.

PLEASE, SIT DOWN.

EXPLAIN YOUR *TARDY* RETURN TO ME.

MAKE IT GOOD.

IN SHORT... WE *FAILED*, MY MINISTER.

THE MINISTER OF MERIDIAN'S SHIP WAS SPEARED...

...BUT SHE WAS NOT SECURED TO IT.

WE WERE UNABLE TO STOP HER.

SHE...FELL.

YOU'RE TELLING ME SHE'S... *DEAD?!*

SEPHIE'S... GONE.

I'M... STAGGERED.

NO, DON'T GET UP. I NEED TO MAKE YOU UNDERSTAND SOMETHING...

YOU *DO* REALIZE WHAT AN *ASTOUNDING* FAILURE THIS REPRESENTS?

PERHAPS THE TOUCH OF MY HAND ON YOUR SHOULDER...

...OR THE *POWER* THAT HAND WIELDS...

...WILL PROVIDE A *REMINDER* TO YOU...

...TO BE MORE *CAREFUL* IN THE FUTURE!

AAAAAHH

BOSCAU, LOROSI... ...MY INTERVIEW WITH THE CAPTAIN IS OVER...

GNNNH!

...CLEAN UP THE MESS.

Oh, IDERIA...

...FORGIVE ME.

I'VE DESTROYED THE LAST OF YOU...

...STUPID, STUBBORN GIRL...

TAKE THIS, JAD.

I KNOW WHAT THEY PACKED YOUR SHIP WITH, AND IT'S FORTIFYING, BUT NOTHING SPECIAL.

THANKS...

...MOM.

Oh, YOU! BE CAREFUL THERE IN CADADOR!

FIND HER QUICKLY AND GET AWAY JUST AS FAST! NOW, GO!

WAIT!

JAD, DON'T LEAVE BEFORE WE...

...GET OUR CHANCE TO WISH YOU GOOD JOURNEY!

IT'S SO BRAVE...

...YOU GOING OFF ALONE TO... RESCUE SEPHIE.

I HAVE TO BE BRAVE.

IT'LL BE DANGEROUS.

IF THE SOLDIERS OF CADADOR CATCH ME --

JAD...

YA!!!!

THERE'S ONE NOW...

...AND YOU'RE HIS PRISONER!

DID I INTERRUPT?

I JUST CAME BY TO REMIND YOU TO STAY OUT OF TROUBLE IN CAPADOR.

MEET UP WITH US AT RING CITY AS SOON AS YOU CAN.

SURE, DAD...

HEE HEE HEE HEE HEE HEE HEE HEE HEE HEE HEE HEE

IF YOU CAN'T FIND HER, LEAVE A MESSAGE AND MOVE ON.

JAD --

-- DON'T PUT YOURSELF IN UNNECESSARY DANGER...

...PLEASE...

...BECAUSE NO ONE COULD REPLACE YOU.

I'LL BE CAREFUL, DAD.

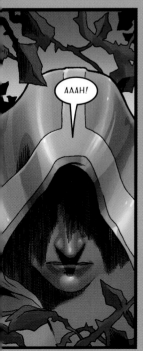

AAAH!

IT'S HEALTHY?

The woman who found me...

She saw the miracle before I did.

The land beyond her city had been blighted for centuries and now part of it had been restored when I appeared.

She made the connection right away...

Oh, YOU POOR CHILD!

CAN YOU STAND?

I THINK SO.

WHO ARE YOU?

HOW DID YOU... Ah, TELL ME LATER.

FOR NOW, LET'S GET YOU TO A PLACE WHERE YOU CAN REST.

QUICKLY, BEFORE IT IS DARK AND THE MONSTERS COME OUT...

Chapter 6

When Stevie Met Sephie

In the first seven issues of *Meridian*, Sephie wasn't the only one who had to do some growing up fast. Associate penciler Steve McNiven, only months into his training at CrossGen's studios, got the call to step up to the majors with *Meridian* #6 and #7.

Asked to chip in with a few pages of *Meridian* #6 to fill in for departing penciler Josh Middleton, Steve was surprised to discover shortly afterward that he would be taking over as the full-time penciler on the book. For a guy who had been working as a professional in comic books for only six months, it was both an unexpected reward and a daunting challenge.

"Two things made it clear that Steve would be an immensely strong penciler on *Meridian*," said writer Barbara Kesel. "Number one, he had a nice way of getting across youth with all of his characters, so I knew he could capture Sephie's younger, rounder features. Number two, he clearly enjoyed adding detail and nuance to the characters' surroundings, and in *Meridian* the environment is every bit as much a character as the cast."

And environment is what Steve immediately gravitated toward as an artist.

"One of the things that stood out to me was background," Steve said. "This is a very different world than most comic book readers are used to, and I wanted to show what it looked like. A lot of comic books are set in places that are familiar, like New York City, but it's different when you have a world where there are floating rocks and logs. Everyone knows what New York City looks like, but no

---

"One of the biggest challenges after being given the assignment of taking over the book was to make *Meridian* reflective of my style without alienating the existing fans..."

---

one's seen a world with physics like this before, so I decided to really work on the backgrounds. I was trying to get a sense of scope by placing the characters in a well-defined environment, and there was a lot there to work from. One of the great draws in *Meridian* is the setting. There is a lot of richness and fuel for the imagination."

Aside from tackling this strange new world like a linebacker downing a scrambling quarterback, Steve also took on the daunting task of inheriting a title after another artist had already established a look and feel for the characters and their world.

"One of the biggest challenges after being given the assignment of taking over the book was to make *Meridian* reflective of my style without alienating the existing fans of the book," Steve said. "In issue #6, when I drew some fill-in pages, I wanted to match Josh's style somewhat so that turning from one of Josh's pages to one of mine didn't jar the fans; when you are starting off with a new book, you want to try to catch the essence of the characters but still be true to the source material. You also want to establish your own style, but you want readers who are used to another artist's style to still recognize the characters. It's a tightrope, and I'm a big guy, so it was a little scary at first, but Barbara wrote a really good script. A lot of interesting things happen at a time when Sephie is beginning to learn a lot more about her powers, so that made it more fun."

LAST NIGHT, AS YOU WERE SUFFERING THROUGH THE TRAUMA OF YOUR...LANDFALL...

...I UNDERSTOOD YOU TO SAY YOU WERE THE MINISTER OF MERIDIAN.

BUT I'VE MET TUROS.

I'M HIS DAUGHTER.

MY FATHER... DIED, VERY RECENTLY.

I AM MINISTER NOW.

Maraya, the Minister of Akasia, was so welcoming. The people were all so kind. They made me want to stay there forever.

The city seemed as warm as the dyes Akasia is known for...

...I know better now.

EEYEW.

SO...A SHIP FROM MERIDIAN BROUGHT YOU HERE?

NO... A SHIP FROM CAPADOR. I WAS STAYING WITH MY UNCLE ILAHN, BUT I'M ON MY WAY HOME NOW.

I'VE NEVER BEEN TO A SURFACE CITY BEFORE.

THEN YOU MUST HAVE A FULL TOUR.

WEAVER'S GUILD...

...WE'RE NOT RICH LIKE CAPADOR, BUT OUR DYES KEEP US PROSPEROUS IN OUR OWN WAY.

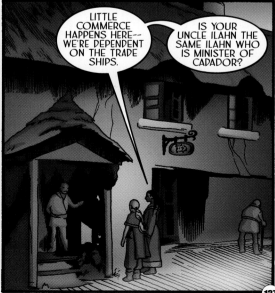

LITTLE COMMERCE HAPPENS HERE-- WE'RE DEPENDENT ON THE TRADE SHIPS.

IS YOUR UNCLE ILAHN THE SAME ILAHN WHO IS MINISTER OF CAPADOR?

YES, THAT'S HIM.

Hmmmm...

AS YOU KNOW, THE SURFACE IS MORE TREACHEROUS THAN THE SKY CITIES, BUT WE OF AKASIA HAVE FORGED A BALANCE BETWEEN DANGER AND VALUE.

WE FLOAT LIKE YOUR CITIES, BUT NOT ON ROCKS-- WE KEEP OUR ANCIENT CONNECTION TO THE GROUND.

THE CATACLYSM MAY HAVE POISONED THE LAND, BUT THOSE SAME TOXINS ACT AS MORDANTS FOR OUR DYES.

ISN'T IT DANGEROUS?

SOMEWHAT, BUT ALL WORK POSES SOME DANGER.

THE REWARDS ARE MANY-- SINCE OUR OWN BIRTH RATES ARE LOW, WE ARE EVEN ABLE TO TAKE IN FOUNDLING CHILDREN FROM ALL OVER DEMETRIA!

MY FAMILY DOES THAT. WE'VE ALWAYS GIVEN A HOME TO...

...ORPHANS.

When we talked about the orphans, my stomach lurched.

Papa's death meant that word now included me.

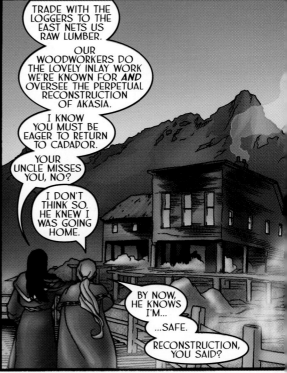

TRADE WITH THE LOGGERS TO THE EAST NETS US RAW LUMBER.

OUR WOODWORKERS DO THE LOVELY INLAY WORK WE'RE KNOWN FOR *AND* OVERSEE THE PERPETUAL RECONSTRUCTION OF AKASIA.

I KNOW YOU MUST BE EAGER TO RETURN TO CADADOR.

YOUR UNCLE MISSES YOU, NO?

I DON'T THINK SO. HE KNEW I WAS GOING HOME.

BY NOW, HE KNOWS I'M...

...SAFE.

RECONSTRUCTION, YOU SAID?

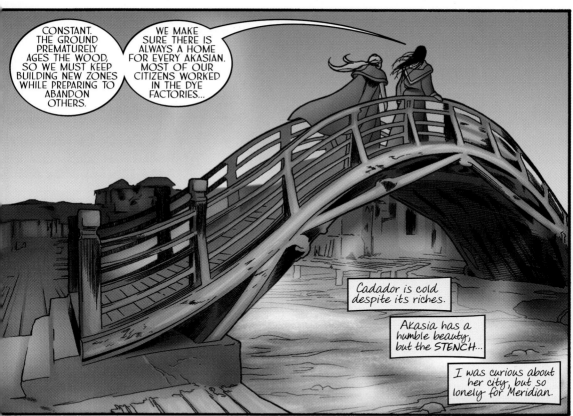

CONSTANT. THE GROUND PREMATURELY AGES THE WOOD, SO WE MUST KEEP BUILDING NEW ZONES WHILE PREPARING TO ABANDON OTHERS.

WE MAKE SURE THERE IS ALWAYS A HOME FOR EVERY AKASIAN. MOST OF OUR CITIZENS WORKED IN THE DYE FACTORIES...

Cadador is cold despite its riches.

Akasia has a humble beauty, but the STENCH...

I was curious about her city, but so lonely for Meridian.

THERE'S NO WAY TO BALANCE THE EQUATION? BUILD STRUCTURES THAT WITHSTAND THE EROSION?

THE DECAYING ZONES ARE NOT BEAUTIFUL, BUT IT'S MORE COST-EFFICIENT TO KEEP BUILDING THAN TO SHORE UP THE PARTS THAT HAVE DECAYED.

WE MUST ALWAYS MOVE FORWARD AND ABANDON THE PAST.

AKASIA PALES NEXT TO CADADOR, BUT IT IS OUR HOME, AND THE MINISTER OF MERIDIAN IS WELCOME TO STAY HERE FOR AS LONG AS IT TAKES HER TO REST FROM HER GRUELING JOURNEY.

PLEASE, THINK OF THIS AS YOUR HOME.

THANK YOU. THAT'S SO KIND.

HOW COULD WE DO LESS FOR A SPECIAL VISITOR FROM...

YES, LOROSI?

MINISTER ILAHN, I MAY HAVE --

I HAVE --

MAY I HAVE --?

THE POINT, LOROSI.

COME TO IT QUICKLY.

THE WOMAN I SPOKE TO YOU OF YESTERDAY?

SHE'S HERE NOW...

...BUT I WILL OF COURSE SEND HER AWAY.

NOT A GOOD TIME.

ABSOLUTELY NOT!

SEND HER IN.

I KEEP MY WORD AND MY APPOINTMENTS.

GOOD.

I ADMIRE THAT IN MY TEACHERS.

"...ALTHOUGH THE HEIR IS NOT AS LOST AS HE IMAGINES."

WHY ARE THEY RUNNING?

Oh, NO. TO HIGH GROUND! *QUICKLY!*

CELANAUG!

THEY'RE FERAL TOXIN-DWELLERS -- BUT IT'S DAYLIGHT!

HURRY -- WE MUST STAY TO THE GOOD AREAS!

NO, SEPHIE -- *THIS* WAY.

BUT, LOOK!

Realization of the danger posed by the monsters of Akasia reached my brain too late...

...my heart had already gone out to the child caught in its path.

I'd never been fearful.

Papa even described me as reckless...

SEPHIE, NO!

WE CAN'T LOSE *YOU!*

YOU WON'T!

...but the feeling that hit me, seeing that boy in danger...

KRA CRAK K

...the sudden fire inside me came from someplace new...

JUMP!

...and there was NOTHING that was going to stop me from saving him!

Suddenly, I was more than Sephie! I was a mythic goddess of protection!

While I was filled with life and strength, no other lives would be lost!

No matter what kind of monsters I had to face.

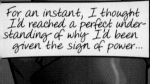

For an instant, I thought I'd reached a perfect understanding of why I'd been given the sign of power...

KERAAAK

...a vision that slipped out of my head as the decaying boards under my feet gave way...

AAAH!

KRUNCH

...and I felt my confidence drop down past my feet into the pit.

Until I spotted the celahaug's cold eyes below...

No snarly-faced toxin-licker was going to stop ME!

This time, when I MADE it happen, I was AWARE of the power coming from me...

...I could feel the fibers repairing themselves...

...as I FORCED it all whole again!

The monster couldn't break through good wood...

...so I poured everything I had inside into creating an avenue of escape...

...one step ahead of the monster.

BYOOM

HOW MANY? THREE?

AND IN DAYLIGHT...

THEY'RE GETTING BOLDER.

The attack left me thrilled at the potential of my new power, and ready to sleep for a week.

THANK YOU, BUT WHY? HOW?

I -- huh...

...JUST DID -- huh...

...huh...

...WHAT WAS RIGHT TO DO.

huh

huh

huh

It also left me feeling I'd grown two heads and a furry tail, the way they all STARED.

...WE HEARD 'LL ABOUT WHAT HAPPENED TO SEPHIE.

ILAHN'S SENT MESSENGERS TO ALL THE CITIES --

-- NO ONE'S TO GIVE HER ANY ASSISTANCE.

AND THE MOUTHPIECES DIDN'T COME ALONE...

...SINCE WE'RE THE CLOSEST TO MERIDIAN, THEY SENT A SQUAD OF CADADORIAN SOLDIERS TO KEEP US HONEST.

THEY'RE ALL OVER THE CITY, "KEEPING THE PEACE."

NOTHING LIKE THE WAY I HEAR THEY DID ON YOUR ISLAND, BUT WE'RE KEEPING CAREFUL.

SINCE WE ALWAYS PROMISED TO HAVE YOU, WE'D NEVER TURN YOU AWAY...

SSWZZZT

...BUT RING CITY CAN'T RISK TAKING IN MERIDIANITES RIGHT NOW...

...SO WE NEED TO HIDE YOU IN PLAIN SIGHT...

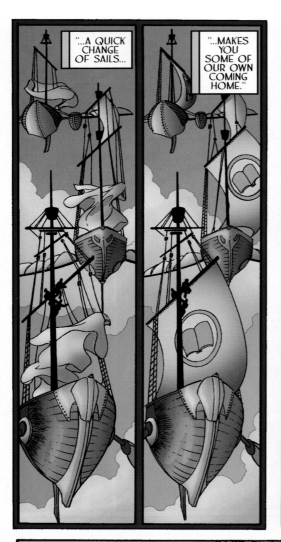

"...A QUICK CHANGE OF SAILS...

"...MAKES YOU SOME OF OUR OWN COMING HOME."

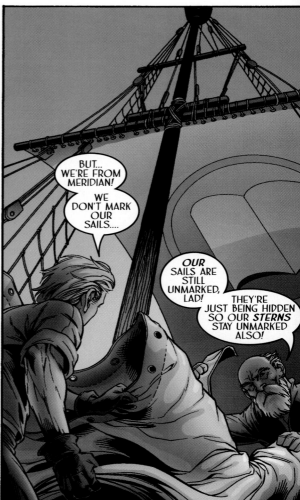

BUT... WE'RE FROM MERIDIAN! WE DON'T MARK OUR SAILS....

OUR SAILS ARE STILL UNMARKED, LAD! THEY'RE JUST BEING HIDDEN SO OUR STERNS STAY UNMARKED ALSO!

BUT, MIRA, IT'S -- WRONG!

SOMETIMES THE WORLD GOES WRONG, ENOS. MAYBE RIGHT NOW WE MUST HIDE WHO WE ARE...

...BUT THAT DOESN'T MEAN WE'LL FORGET.

THE GIRL LET THINGS SLIP IN HER DELIRIUM LAST NIGHT.

NO SHIP BROUGHT HER --

-- SEPHIE OF MERIDIAN FELL FROM THE AIR AND *DID NOT DIE.*

THIS WAS WITNESSED BY ILAHN'S SOLDIERS, SO ILAHN MUST BELIEVE HER DEAD.

DOES THAT HAVE SOMETHING TO DO WITH THIS REJUVENATION?

YES.

SHE DID IT.

YOU SAW WHAT SHE DID AGAINST THE CELANAUG.

I BROUGHT YOU OUT HERE TO ADVISE ME IN A DECISION:

DO WE ENTICE SEPHIE TO STAY?

KEEP THE GIRL IN AKASIA, HIDDEN, OR SEND A MESSENGER TO CADADOR?

CHEATING ILAHN'S A DANGER.

KEEP HER!

IF ILAHN BELIEVES HER DEAD, HE'LL NEVER LOOK FOR HER HERE!

WE SIMPLY... FAIL TO NOTIFY.

IF HIS SPIES EVER DISCOVER HER, TRADE SHIPS COULD SKIP OUR PORT.

DON'T FORGET HIS BLOCKADE OF SEGEN OR WHAT HE'S THREATENING TO DO TO TORBEL...

...LET IT *FALL.*

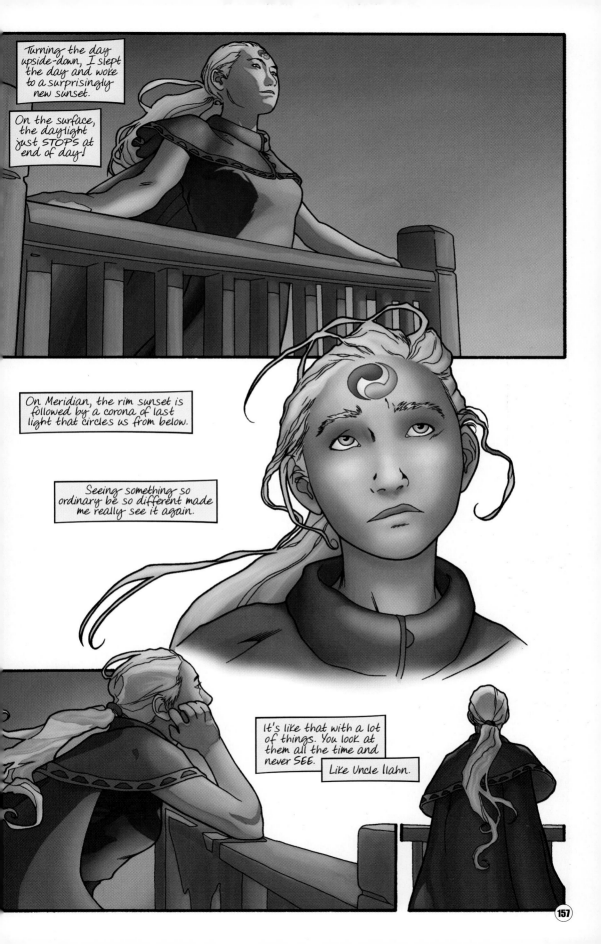

Turning the day upside-down, I slept the day and woke to a surprisingly new sunset.

On the surface, the daylight just STOPS at end of day!

On Meridian, the rim sunset is followed by a corona of last light that circles us from below.

Seeing something so ordinary be so different made me really see it again.

It's like that with a lot of things. You look at them all the time and never SEE.

Like Uncle Ilahn.

Sunset had never been more to me than a cue to go home, but that night it became a living symbol of my promise to Meridian.

Ilahn of Cadador would NOT destroy my island.

I'd do something good for the people of Akasia to repay them for their kindness, but then it was time for me to go home...

...and start a war.

Chapter 7

"We're just beginning to lay the groundwork of the bigger story of Demetria's ological decline. The need for commerce will have to be alanced against he decay of the planet itself."

– Barbara Kesel

Sephie and Ilahn: Compressed Conflict

Only Sephie could pull off this little piece of dialogue.

At the end of Chapter Six, Sephie spreads her arms to the sky, and in the background is a spectacular blue and purple and red and yellow sunset – an image of beauty and promise. And her last line of dialogue?

"…it was time for me to go home and start a war."

But that is the compressed conflict that is built into nearly every layer of *Meridian*. Sephie is the spring, while Ilahn is winter. Meridian is craft, while Cadador is commerce. Demetria itself is a world in the constant throes of decay and renewal. With all these contrasting ideas, the challenge for the creative team was to craft a book that could portray the chaos that Sephie's life had become without losing the beauty of her soul.

"When we asked (*Meridian* penciler) Josh Middleton to design the characters, the idea was to make the entire cast very identifiable," said CrossGen art director Brandon Peterson. "Sephie was created as typically pretty, sweet, and spunky. Everything about her immediate family was bright. Her father was practically Santa Claus, with the big, friendly, fatherly white beard and the softness around the middle."

But flip the coin over, and there is the dark side of Demetria: the Cadadorian Minister, Ilahn.

"For Ilahn, we went in the opposite direction," Brandon explained. "Very dark, menacing, pessimistic – basically the antithesis of what Sephie is. He is scarred physically, emotionally, and spiritually, so we portrayed him as mutilated and gangly and thin, showing decay and wickedness. While Sephie

---

"The world of *Meridian* is a strange dichotomy. It's a world in constant upheaval, in a state of decay and lapse, but we didn't want to show just the decay. We wanted to show the natural beauty of this place."

---

prefers pastel colors for her clothes, Ilahn prefers dark colors. He wears heavy, somber robes with weighty metal dragging him down even more."

Even the ecological/ economic backdrop portrays a pattern of conflict. "This series is really a parable about commerce," according to *Meridian* writer Barbara Kesel.

"Everything in *Meridian* ha to do with economic realitie The money story is coupled with the ticking clock of an environmental disaster in th making – the escalating pattern of consumption is accelerating the decay of th world. We're just beginning lay the groundwork of the bigger story of Demetria's ecological decline. The need for commerce will have to balanced against the decay the planet itself. It's all abou resources: money, time, people, fuel, and food. And when it comes to resources Sephie has plenty to draw upon."

And the challenge for Brandon and the art team was to figure out a way to portray these themes throu the art of *Meridian* without hitting the reader over the head with the messages.

"The world of *Meridia* is a strange dichotomy," said Brandon. "It's a world in constant upheaval, in a state of decay and lapse, but we didn't want to show just the decay. We wanted t show the natural beauty o this place. Designing thing from the cities that float in the sky to the ships that carry people to and from them – there is a sense of age and beauty, like an antique piece of hand- crafted furniture."

The economy of Akasia revolves around a cycle of decay.

They rebuild the city at one end and abandon the other as ground toxins eat it away.

It's a business decision: construction is cheaper than prevention... ...and Akasia is poor.

Growing up on Meridian, I didn't know what kind of disease "poor" was, only that surface people had it:

When they earned enough to recover, they moved up to the sky cities.

I never joined Papa on journeys to the surface...

...I was afraid I'd catch the disease.

And now, I was its cure.

Reaching out with my fingers I could feel what needed to be fixed and find the power to make it right.

The mark on my head gave me a gift.

Papa's love taught me to share.

Although he'd wink and point out that creating goodwill IS good business.

They touched me and the toxins burned THEM...

...but I was fine.

Perfectly fine.

All these unusual abilities...

...what was I turning into?

Was I really Sephie anymore?

SEPHIE...

...YOU ARE...

...A VERY UNUSUAL CHILD.

...THAT'S NOT HOW WE DID IT ON MERIDIAN.

BUT YOU'RE NOT ON MERIDIAN...

...YOU'RE IN *RING CITY* NOW.

AND WE HAVE OUR OWN WAYS OF COAXING WORN EQUIPMENT BACK INTO SERVICE.

IF YOU'D JUST SERVICE YOUR MACHINES MORE FAITHFULLY, YOU'D SEE BETTER SERVICE FROM THEM!

GENTLEMEN! GENTLEWOMEN! SORRY TO INTERRUPT. I'M MINISTER ODWIN. WELCOME TO RING CITY!

I'M SORRY WE HAD TO HUSTLE YOU ALL INTO HERE, BUT YOU UNDERSTAND THE *SITUATION* WITH CADADOR.

TAKARTY, CAN I SPEAK WITH YOU... ...PRIVATELY?

JON, I RECOGNIZE THAT YOU AND YOURS HAVE HAD TO GIVE UP EVERYTHING TO LEAVE MERIDIAN...

...AND I DON'T WANT TO ADD WEIGHT TO YOUR BURDEN...

...BUT I'VE A RESPONSIBILITY TO MY CITYMATES TO ASK YOU THIS:

WHAT ARE YOUR PLANS, JON? ARE YOU GOING TO *STAY* IN RING CITY?

YOU'RE ALL WELCOME TO LIVE HERE -- WE'VE PLENTY OF ROOM -- BUT WE CAN'T CONTINUE TO HIDE YOU AWAY.

THERE'S BOUND TO BE A SLIP.

WE'LL PROTECT YOU FOR AS LONG AS POSSIBLE, BUT I HAVE TO WATCH OVER OUR CITY'S SECURITY...

"...BECAUSE CADADORIAN SOLDIERS LURK EVERYWHERE."

169

THOSE LAND-LOCKED CADADORIAN SOLDIERS WON'T THINK TO LOOK *UP* IF WE'RE *QUIET!*

WHERE'S THE BOY?

NO, HE'S DISAPPEARED!

JUST AHEAD.

I'VE GOT HELP EVERYWHERE! *GREAT* SAVE.

I OWE YOU A BIG ONE.

WENT THA'WAY. KEEP GOIN'.

THIS WAY!

AFTER HIM!

DON'T FRET IT.

I'VE HAD TO RUN FROM CADADORIAN SOLDIERS A TIME OR TWO MYSELF...

YOU SEE THE MARK UPON MY THROAT?

THE SIGIL WAS A GIFT TO ME FROM AN UNKNOWN SOURCE.

IT CAME WITH NO INSTRUCTION, NO DEMANDS FOR PAYMENT...

...ALTHOUGH IT'S EARLY YET TO TELL IF COST WILL ACCOMPANY ITS OBVIOUS ADVANTAGES.

IT MAKES YOU IMPERVIOUS TO PAIN?

Oh, NO. I STILL FEEL PAIN...

...BUT I TRANSCEND THE SENSATION...

...BECAUSE I HAVE BECOME ONE WITH *DESTRUCTION*...

...AND DESTRUCTION ENDS ALL PAIN.

BUT NOT *ALL* FEELING?

NO.

NOK NOK

MINISTER ILAHN?

THERE'S A MESSENGER FROM *AKASIA.* NEWS ABOUT--

IT'S A *PERSONAL* MESSAGE.

SEPHIE, THE PEOPLE OF AKASIA WILL ALWAYS HOLD YOU IN THEIR HEARTS FOR YOUR ACT OF KINDNESS.

INSPIRED BY YOUR TREATMENT OF ME! LIKE FOR LIKE!

SEPHIE...

WOULD YOU CONSIDER STAYING IN AKASIA?

THE GOOD YOU'VE DONE WILL SOON BE UNDONE BY THE TOXINS...

I UNDERSTAND.

YOU HAVE A CITY TO CARE FOR...

I'D LOVE TO STAY HERE AND KEEP AKASIA HEALTHY.

BUT I HAVE A BIGGER RESPONSIBILITY, TO GO HOME AND TAKE CARE OF MY CITY.
AS A FELLOW MINISTER, I KNOW YOU'LL UNDERSTAND MY DUTY TO MERIDIAN.
I HAVE TO LEAVE.
Oh, YES...
...I...
YES...I UNDERSTAND.
YOU MUST DO WHAT'S BEST FOR ***MERIDIAN.***
AS I MUST DO WHAT IS BEST FOR AKASIA...

BEFORE YOU LEAVE US, SEPHIE...

...THERE'S STILL A PART OF AKASIA YOU HAVEN'T SEEN.

YOU'VE SEEN OUR CRAFTS. LET ME GIVE YOU A TOUR OF OUR INDUSTRY.

I'D LIKE THAT!

GUARD, PASS ON A MESSAGE FOR ME...

YES, MY MINISTER.

I'M ALWAYS CURIOUS TO SEE HOW OTHER CITIES WORK.

THIS IS WHERE YOUR DYES ARE PROCESSED?

YES, AND WE'RE RATHER PROUD OF THE INNOVATIVE WAY WE KEEP IT COST-EFFICIENT...

AAAAH!

IT'S RUN BY CHILDREN?!

There's a famous painting in Cadador.

It's an image of a beautiful woman cradling a child.

When you look again, you see a terrible beast, snarling and about to strike.

Once you spot the beast, you can never see the beauty again without flinching.

In Akasia that day, I finally saw the beast...

Judging a Cover by Its Look

Making comic books is fun. Selling them is hard, which is why the cover is one of the single most important elements of this business. Introducing a new comic book from a new company with no track record and high expectations, the cover needs to do everything but sing and dance.

Moreover, *Meridian*'s covers needed to convey so much more than a typical comic book cover. There was mood, conflict, environment and distinctive personality that had to shine through in a single image. Far different from a typical superhero comic where the image usually involves one really big guy in a costume trying to beat up another really big guy in a costume, *Meridian*'s covers combined creative function with stylistic form, and they did it in such a way that they didn't give away too much of the story.

"You have to give the reader an idea of what is inside the issue without giving away main story points inappropriately," said CrossGen art director Brandon Peterson. "We sometimes don't use the cover image on the inside of the book exactly as it's portrayed, but it always gives the gist of what's inside."

Meridian writer Barbara Kesel said many of the challenges with *Meridian*'s covers came from the constant battle not to let Sephie fall into the typical "damsel-in-distress" mode. She was a strong character, and the covers needed to show that.

"In the 'movie montage' that we presented on the cover of #1, we didn't show Sephie as a teen-age girl in a party dress," Barbara said. "We showed her in an outfit that presents her more as an adventurer. In issue #2, the cover helped get across the harshness of the big-city environment of Cadador by

---

"We sometimes don't use the cover image on the inside of the book exactly as it's portrayed, but it always gives the gist of what's inside."

---

matching the intricacy of the lace in Sephie's outfit with the gritty quality of statuary and sky. The many layers of texture helped make Cadador more chilling because it became so *real*."

On the cover of #3, the team showed Ilahn in his study, and it gives the first hint of how many floating islands there are in this world as he holds a three-dimensional globe in his hand. "He's holding it but also

destroying it almost unconsciously, showing how much of a cold creature he is," Barbara added. "And that cover was a great contrast to the cover of #4, where we go from Ilahn's cold villainy to the bright heroism of Sephie. That cover has proven to be everyone's favorite cover so far, again underscoring the struggle between dark and light in this story."

Barbara expressed some reservations early on about the cover to #5 because of the potential pitfall of showing Sephie in typical girl-comic-character peril.

"Conceptually, I was a little concerned with the cover of #5. I wanted to avoid the cliché of the woman victim with Sephie, but there is no image more disturbing in a world of floating islands than someone falling helplessly through the sky," she said. "Josh did a magnificent job of keeping that cover from being a clichè. And the cover of #6 was another tough task because we wanted to get across the decaying environment of Akasia, but we also needed the up-close horror of Sephie's jeopardy. And finally, Steve McNiven got his turn to shine with the cover of #7, in which Steve provides a terrific sense of mood through not only characters but through his incredible attention to the detail of their environment."

CROSSGEN®

COMICS

offers a full line of monthly comic books for people with discerning tastes. Let CrossGen take you back to a time when heroes didn't have to wear Spandex, capes or masks.

If you like:

- Magic and mysticism, you'll love MYSTIC
- Science fiction, you'll love SIGIL
- Medieval sword and sorcery with a twist, you'll love SCION
- Fairy-tale fantasy, you'll love MERIDIAN
- Larger-than-life gods, you'll love THE FIRST
- Apocalyptic science fantasy, you'll love CRUX
- Tolkien-esque high fantasy, you'll love SOJOURN

Join the ever-growing community of comic book readers. For a taste, log on to www.crossgen.com and explore our worlds, read our message boards, or chat with other fans in our chat rooms. These comics aren't JUST for kids!

To find a comic book store in your area, call 1-888-comicbook. Or log on to http://csls.diamondcomics.com

You'll be glad you did!

www. CROSSGEN® .com
COMICS